LADDER

AX

PIKE POLE

SHOVEL

NOZZLE

HOSE

CHAIN SAW

FIRE HYDRANT

For Tien and Reid

Copyright © 2015 by Mike Austin

All rights reserved. Published in the United States by Random House Children's Books, a division of Random House LLC, a Penguin Random House Company, New York.

Random House and the colophon are registered trademarks of Random House LLC.

Visit us on the Web! randomhousekids.com

Educators and librarians, for a variety of teaching tools, visit us at RHTeachersLibrarians.com

Library of Congress Cataloging-in-Publication Data
Austin, Mike, author, illustrator.
Fire engine no. 9 / by Mike Austin. — First edition.
  pages cm.
Summary: Follows a fire engine and its crew through a very busy day, using mainly sound words.
ISBN 978-0-553-51095-9 (trade) — ISBN 978-0-375-97428-1 (lib. bdg.) — ISBN 978-0-553-51096-6 (ebook)
[1. Fire engines—Fiction. 2. Fire fighters—Fiction.] I. Title. II. Title: Fire engine number nine.   PZ7.A9253Fir 2015   [E]—dc23 2014016610

MANUFACTURED IN CHINA   10 9 8 7 6 5 4 3 2 1   First Edition

FIRE ENGINE No. 9

by Mike Austin

Random House 🏠 New York

ALERT! ALERT!

FIRE!

FIRE!

FIRE!

WHOOSH WHOOSH

WEOOO! WEOOO! WEOOO!

HONK! HONK! HONK!

ENGINE NO. 9

LUIGI'S

CLIMB! CLIMB! CLIMB!

CRAWL! CRAWL!

Hooray!
Hooray!

ALL NEW! Mobile Lunch Buffet!

LUIGI'S *on* WHEELS!

Eat!
Eat!

Pasta! Meatballs!
Pizza! Calzones!
Ravioli! Lasagna!

Thank you,
ENGINE No.9

WE'RE BACK!

BEEP! BEEP! BEEP! BEEP! BEEP! BEEP!

What to Do During a Home Fire*

- Get low and go! Crawl under smoke to an exit. Heavy smoke and deadly gases collect along the ceiling.

- If you hear a smoke alarm, get out fast! You may only have a few seconds to escape.

- If smoke is blocking the door, use your second way out of the room or house.

- Feel the doorknob and door before opening it. If either is hot, leave the door closed and use the second way out.

- If you see smoke coming around the door, use the second way out.

- If you do open a door, open it slowly and be ready to shut it quick if there's smoke.

- Don't hide from firefighters! They may look scary with all of their equipment, but they are there to help you.

- Tell firefighters if there are any pets trapped in the house. Don't try to get them yourself!

- If your clothes catch on fire, stop, drop, and roll! Stop, drop to the ground, and cover your face with your hands. Then roll over and over or back and forth until the fire is out.

*Text is from "Be a Hero!" Federal Emergency Management Agency (FEMA), ready.gov/kids/know-the-facts/home-fires.

Get low and go!

HELMET

SMOKE ALARM

FIRST-AID KIT

BOOTS

FIRE EXTINGUISHER

WALKIE-TALKIE

BULLHORN

FLASHLIGHT

GLOVES